Charlie
the Cheerful

Based on *The Railway Series* by the Rev. W. Awdry

Illustrations by *Robin Davies and Nigel Chilvers*

EGMONT

EGMONT

We bring stories to life

First published in Great Britain 2010
This edition published in 2011
by Egmont UK Limited
The Yellow Building, 1 Nicholas Road, London W11 4AN

Thomas the Tank Engine & Friends™

CREATED BY BRITT ALLCROFT

HiT entertainment

ISBN 978 1 4052 5115 0
46671/9
Printed in Italy

FSC
MIX
Paper
FSC® C018306

Egmont is passionate about helping to preserve the world's remaining ancient forests.
We only use paper from legal and sustainable forest sources.

This book is made from paper certified by the Forestry Stewardship Council® (FSC®),
an organisation dedicated to promoting responsible management of forest resources.
For more information on the FSC, please visit www.fsc.org. To learn more about
Egmont's sustainable paper policy, please visit www.egmont.co.uk/ethical

Percy smiled at Thomas' excited face. "I have some news, too," he peeped. "Someone else is arriving at the Docks today."

"Who?" Thomas asked, puzzled.

"Charlie, the new engine!" Percy laughed. "He's the Mainland Controller's favourite. Everyone says he's the most fun engine ever, even more than you!"

Before Thomas could reply, Percy had chuffed cheerfully away.

"Bumpers and buffers!" thought Thomas. "I didn't think any engine could be more fun than me." He puffed off to meet Alicia Botti at the Docks, his wheels whirring with worry.

"I'm so pleased to be travelling with you, Thomas," she said as she boarded Annie.

Thomas felt very proud until he saw a small engine, painted a cheeky bright purple. "That must be Charlie!" Thomas whistled, quietly.

"He's smaller than me, and he certainly doesn't look more fun than me!" thought Thomas, frowning.

The purple engine puffed up with a mischievous smile. "Hello, I'm Charlie. Are you Thomas?"

When Thomas said yes, Charlie continued, "I've heard a lot about you. The Mainland engines say you're even more fun than me."

Thomas was very surprised!

Just then, The Fat Controller arrived. "Thomas, Charlie has a busy first day on Sodor," he boomed. "He's helping with the Concert. He has to collect the ice cream from the Dairy and the red carpet from Knapford Station. Will you look after him?"

"Yes, Sir," replied Thomas.

"Yippee!" whistled Charlie with a burst of steam.

The Fat Controller chuckled as he left.

"Let's race to the Dairy!" Charlie chirped, cheekily.

"I'm too busy for races today," Thomas replied.

"I heard you were a fun engine," Charlie tooted.
"But you're not fun at all."

Thomas didn't like being told he wasn't fun.
"All right," he said. "I'll race you to the Dairy, then
I'll take Miss Botti to the Town Hall. I'm sure there
is time," he decided.

And with a flash in their fireboxes, the race was on!

Thomas and Charlie roared through tunnels and thundered through junctions, laughing all the way. When they reached the Dairy, Thomas had beaten Charlie by a single buffer!

"How exciting that was!" trilled Alicia Botti. She sang a lovely song that made everyone smile.

"If you were a really fun engine, you'd race me to Knapford next," panted Charlie as his ice-cream churns were loaded.

Thomas wasn't sure. He was late, but he wanted Charlie to think that he was a fun engine. "One more race, Charlie . . ." he agreed.

The two engines wheeshed off again. Halfway to Knapford Station, Thomas saw Gordon huffing towards the Town Hall with The Fat Controller.

"Cinders and ashes! I'm very late!" Thomas gasped. "Miss Botti will miss her own Concert!"

He whistled goodbye to Charlie, then sped away down the line. It was a very bumpy ride, and his couplings became looser with every rattle.

As he bumped on to the bridge, his coupling hook went SNAP! But in his rush, Thomas didn't notice he had left Annie and Clarabel behind.

At the Town Hall, Thomas steamed to a stop. "Here I am, Sir!" he whistled to The Fat Controller, who was waiting on the platform.

The Fat Controller looked at Thomas, sternly. "Here *you* are, Thomas," he boomed. "But where are Annie and Clarabel with Miss Botti?"

Thomas' Driver looked behind and had a terrible shock – the two carriages were missing! Thomas had been having fun, when he should have been being Really Useful.

"I'm sorry, Sir. I'll go and find them, straight away!" Thomas said.

Thomas puffed quickly back the way he had come. At a junction, he saw Charlie chuffing up and told him the problem.

"Let's have a race to find your carriages," Charlie tooted. "The winner will be the Number One Fun Engine!"

Thomas frowned. "No, Charlie. I want to be a Really Useful Engine more than I want to be a fun one."

When the signal changed, Thomas crossed the junction and steamed away.

Thomas was very worried as he puffed along. Suddenly, he heard someone singing. "That's Miss Botti's lovely voice!" he thought, happily.

He puffed up to the bridge. Miss Botti was leaning out of Annie's doorway, singing to a crowd of people below. Thomas had never heard anything so beautiful!

When she had finished her song, Thomas smiled and told her, "I'm sorry I left you behind, but we must go now!"

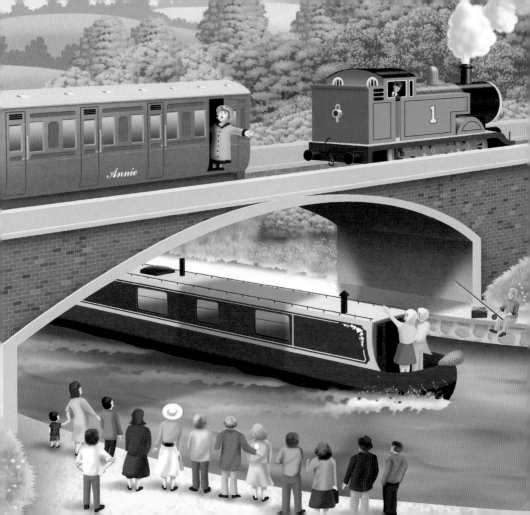

Everyone was waiting for them at the Town Hall Station. Charlie smiled when he saw Thomas puff in with his carriages.

But The Fat Controller looked cross. "You've made Miss Botti very late, Thomas," he said, sternly.

"Not at all, Sir Topham," trilled Alicia Botti. "I've had the ride of my life, with so many people to sing to. Thomas is such fun!"

Thomas was delighted! And he whistled, "Peep! Peep!" to his new fun friend, Charlie.